Licensed exclusively to Top That Publishing Ltd
Tide Mill Way, Woodbridge, Suffolk, IP12 1AP, UK
www.topthatpublishing.com
Copyright © 2014 Tide Mill Media
All rights reserved
0 2 4 6 8 9 7 5 3 1
Printed and bound in China

ISBN 978-1-78244-783-2

A catalogue record for this book is available from the British Library

Little Kitty
and
Little Brown Dog

Meow, meow, purr, mew,

Little Kitty's big round eyes are blue.

She likes to chase a ball around,

And follows it in leaps and bounds.

Meow, meow, purr, mew,
Little Kitty is just like me and you!
On comfy cushions, in a heap
She purrs and has a little sleep.

Meow! Meow!

Meow, meow, purr, mew,
Little Kitty chased a bird and off it flew!
Through the long, tall grass she goes,
And jumps around on tippy-toes.

Meow! Meow!

Meow, meow, purr, mew,
Little Kitty's wet from the morning dew.
Leaving muddy paw prints on the ground,
She heads straight for the milk she's found.

Meow, meow, purr, mew,
Little kitty loves you, do you love her too?
She's the cutest bundle of furry fun,
Who loves to cuddle, play and run.

Woof, bark, woof woof, bark,
Little Brown Dog likes to play in the park.
His furry tummy almost touches the ground,
What a roly-poly, brown little hound.

Woof, bark, woof woof, bark,
Little Brown Dog is scared of the dark!
He's not the bravest dog in the night,
He hides in his bed, in case of a fright.

Woof, bark, woof woof, bark,
Little Brown Dog is in the bath!
His ears are floppy, his eyes are round,
What fun he's having, splashing around!

Woof, bark, woof woof, bark,
Little Brown Dog likes to play in the park
He wants to play with a bug, so small,
But the bug doesn't want to play at all!

Woof, bark, woof woof, bark,
Little Brown Dog will make you laugh!
He's the cutest, cuddliest dog around,
With a loud, happy, woofing-dog sound.